I Love The Night

written & illustrated by
Dar Hosta

Brown Dog Books
Flemington, New Jersey

Published by Brown Dog Books
PO Box 2196 Flemington, NJ 08822

ISBN 0-9721967-0-6

The illustrations in this book were created using collage, oil pastel, colored pencil
and a digital graphics tablet. The type is Century Gothic.

Also by Dar Hosta, *I Love The Alphabet*

Special Thanks:
To my husband, you are my man behind the scenes.
To my family and friends, for your love and encouragement the whole way through.
To Gil Porter, my mentor and my friend, for giving me another A.
To the children, you helped me find this path with your honest praise.
To the grown ups, for supporting my career in the arts over the years.

This book is dedicated
with infinite love
to my Dad

Once upon a time it was night. It was a perfectly perfect time for becoming still and quiet, for making up a good dream, and for floating off to sleep.

But, as the sky began to dim, there was a stirring and a scurrying, a wiggling and a waking; and a whisper on the wind called out, *"I love the night..."*

And the nocturnal adventure began.

A pair of crickets sit at the edge of a quiet pond, beneath a giant willow tree, in the still summer twilight. Night sounds are just starting to be heard. The boy cricket rubs his wings together and begins his sundown song.

"I love the night," he sings. "It is so marvelously marvelous for making moonlight music."

The girl cricket settles herself into the cool evening grass and enjoys his chirping.

"I love the night," she croons. "It is so delightfully delightful for a starry serenade."

A twinkling cloud lights up the sky, as hundreds and thousands of fireflies begin their sparkly nighttime display.

"We love the night," the little beetles call out to each other as they pass in the air. "It is so spectacularly spectacular for flying and for flashing!"

Yellow-green glow on, yellow-green glow off, flashing on, flashing off, into the night, in the firefly light show.

Far below the ocean's rolling waves, a groggy, large-eyed octopus is awakening.

"I love the night," gurgles the octopus. "It is so splendidly splendid for getting some length in the limbs."

He slowly unrolls himself from his deep-sea bed to wander the darkening waters, hoping to scare up a delicious dinner.

High above the ground, in the heart of a beautiful and swampy rain forest, a small green frog with big red eyes is rousing from his daytime slumber, in the cradle of a leaf.

"I love the night," croaks the tiny tree frog. "It is so fabulously fabulous for calling to my companions and for creeping across the canopy."

He finds a frog friend and happily hops off, into the blue-green night, to make some more croaking.

Beneath a crescent moon, floating on a night breeze over a stand of starry-leaved sweet gum trees, a magnificent lime-green luna moth makes her way across the sky.

"I love the night," whispers the graceful and gorgeous moth. "It is so beautifully beautiful for finding just the right leaf for my dainty and delicate eggs."

The luna moth floats gently through the sweet gum leaves until she finds just the perfect leaf.

By the light of a full moon, the nightjars are coursing through the sky, wings fluttering, gliding over the moonlit shadows of old oak trees.

"I love the night," comes from the call of the whip-poor-will. "It is so gloriously glorious for agile aerobatics."

With a loop-the-loop of dips and dives, he soars off, into the night, leaving an echo of *whip-poor-will, whip-poor-will!*

Out of a cozy den in a hollowed out tree, a wily black-masked raccoon comes out to wash her hands in the moonlit forest stream.

"I love the night," giggles the playful ring-tailed raccoon. "It is so enjoyably enjoyable for paddling and for playing!"

The furry raccoon bounds into the bubbling stream where she splishes and splashes all night long.

Perched upon one of the
topmost branches of a
mottled old sycamore tree, a
sleepy horned owl opens one
lazy eye at a time.

"I love the night," mutters the owl.
"It is so superbly superb for getting
some wind under the wings."

The owl gives his head a turn all the way around to the left, and
then gives his head a turn all the way around to the right. With
a mighty flap of his enormous wings, he takes flight, relishing the
feeling of the midnight sky flowing through his feathers.

In a dim corner of the sleeping flower bed, an orange and yellow
spattered garden spider busily mends her web.

"I love the night," proclaims the diligent spider. "It is so wonderfully wonderful for working on my weaving."

The pretty spider keeps two eyes on her work, and the other six on the lookout for the night's supper.

High up in the jungle trees, a multitude of furry fruit bats are waking from their lazy day.

"We love the night," chatter the little bats, circling above the treetops. "It is so magnificently magnificent for a fruit-finding flight!"

The agile night travelers spy some banana trees in the distance and

Below the trees, below the tops of woodland plants, down on the ground, among the fallen leaves and the twigs, a small, shy dormouse crawls out from a snugly nest where she has slept the day away.

"I love the night," squeaks the little dormouse, her large ears twitching this way and that. "The air is so sweetly sweet with the smell of honeysuckle."

She scurries over to a branch, heavy to the ground with flowers,
where she sniffs and snacks, happily, until dawn.

Four golden starfish creep out from behind the rocks in the shallow and shimmering waters of their tide pool.

"We love the night," the starfish chant in perfect chorus. "It is so excellently excellent for finding a cool and comfortable place to wave our arms around."

The starfish inch their way out into the moonshine, little by little. Five arms go this way, five arms go that way, five arms this way, five arms that way, joining together in an aquatic constellation.

"I love the night," says the Moon, as she smiles to herself and looks upon the Earth with a great and glowing love.

She makes up a sweet sounding lullaby for all the sleeping creatures, and for all the waking creatures. She sings to all the quiet creatures, and to all the noisy creatures. She sings to all the still creatures and to all the busy creatures, and she sings to the whole spinning blue and green planet below. She sings a sweet song of peace.

Whirling gently through the Universe, she hums happily ever after.

Sweet dreams...